PK 23/7/07

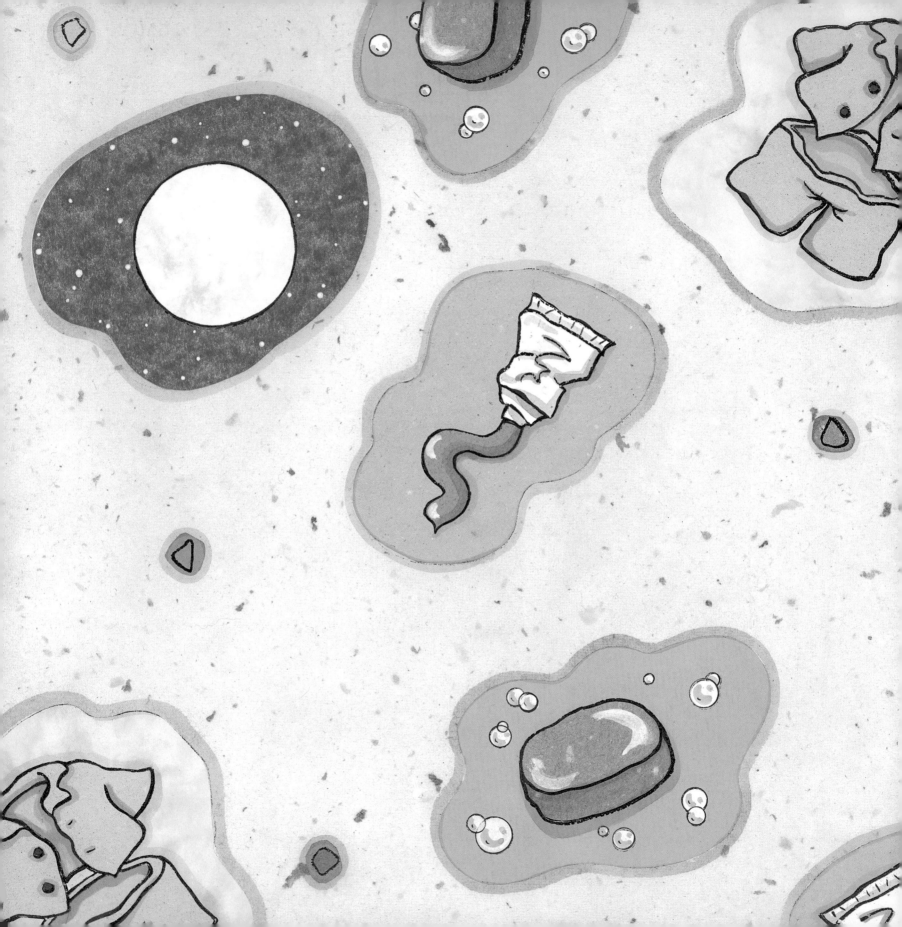

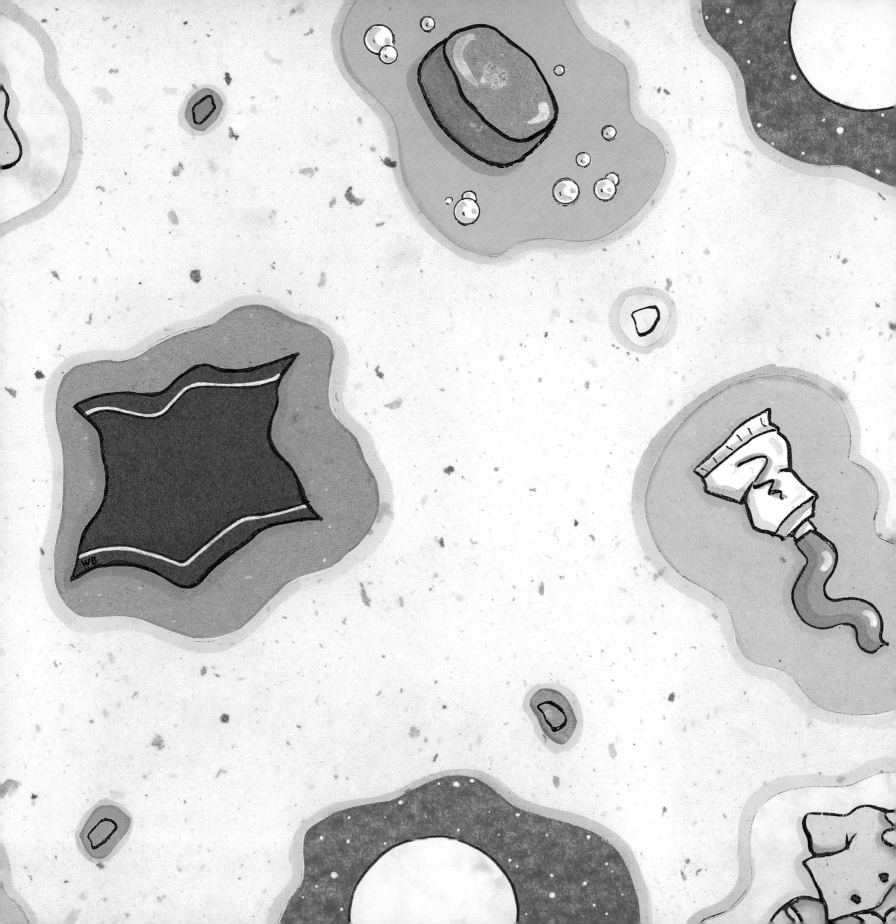

OXFORD
UNIVERSITY PRESS

Great Clarendon Street, Oxford OX2 6DP

Oxford University Press is a department of the University of Oxford.
It furthers the University's objective of excellence in research, scholarship,
and education by publishing worldwide in

Oxford New York

Auckland Bangkok Buenos Aires Cape Town Chennai
Dar es Salaam Delhi Hong Kong Istanbul Karachi Kolkata
Kuala Lumpur Madrid Melbourne Mexico City Mumbai Nairobi
São Paulo Shanghai Taipei Tokyo Toronto

Oxford is a registered trade mark of Oxford University Press
in the UK and in certain other countries

British Library Cataloguing in Publication Data available

ISBN 0-19-279137-0 Hardback
ISBN 0-19-279138-9 Paperback

1 3 5 7 9 10 8 6 4 2

Printed in Italy

Colour reproductions by Dot Gradations Ltd, UK

Wobble Bear says yellow

IAN WHYBROW AND CAROLINE JAYNE CHURCH

OXFORD
UNIVERSITY PRESS

Wobble Bear was bouncing.

(He was bouncing on the bed.)

His mummy caught him in a towel

and this is what she said:

'Now, what colour is the towel, Wobble?'
And Wobble laughed and he said,

'Yellow!'

Mum took him to the bathroom
and she popped him on the sink.

She said,
     'Look, Wobble,
       this soap is
         PINK!

    Now, what colour
       is the soap, Wobble?'

And Wobble said . . .

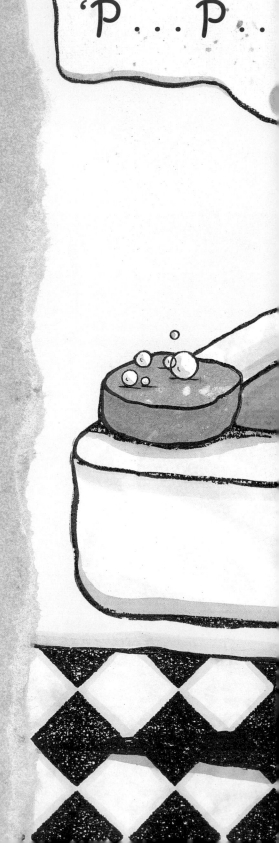

'P . . . P . .

Then Mum picked up
the toothpaste.
She said, 'Hurry,
Wobble, do!'

Out squeezed a squirt that was BLUE, BLUE, **BLUE!**

'Now, Wobble Bear.
No mucking about.
What colour toothpaste
did Mummy squeeze out?'
And Wobble smiled . . .
And Wobble said . . .

'Yellow!'

'Right you cheeky Wobble,
I don't want to have a scene.
Put on your nice
pyjamas that are

GREEN,

GREEN,

GREEN!

Now come along, Wobble!
Tell Mummy.
What colour are
your pyjamas?'

And did Wobble say his pyjamas were green?
Nope.

He said . . .
. . . well you know what he said!

Exactly,
he said,

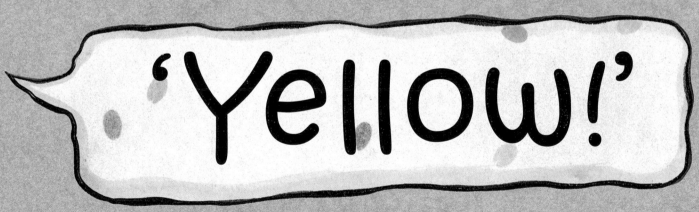

'Yellow!'

Mum said, 'Time for bed,
my funny little fellow.

And take your little teddy
who is really

truly

yellow.'

(Now that was a mistake. She never should have said that.
Because Wobble started calling everything yellow.)

He said 'YELLOW' to his dinosaur,

and 'YELLOW' to his pot.

He said
'YELLOW, YELLOW, YELLOW,'
was the colour of his cot!

He said 'YELLOW' to his wardrobe,

he said 'YELLOW' to his sheep.

He said 'YELLOW' to his welly boots,

and 'YELLOW' to his jeep!

So Mum said, 'Yellow is the only word you know!

'Just settle down and close your eyes and off to sleep you go!'

So Wobble sucked his thumb a bit,
and gave a little sigh.
And Wobble whispered, 'Yellow'
and he pointed to the sky.

Yes, Wobble whispered, 'Yellow.'
And this time, he was right.
The yellow moon said, 'Clever bear!'
And whispered back . . .
'Goodnight.'

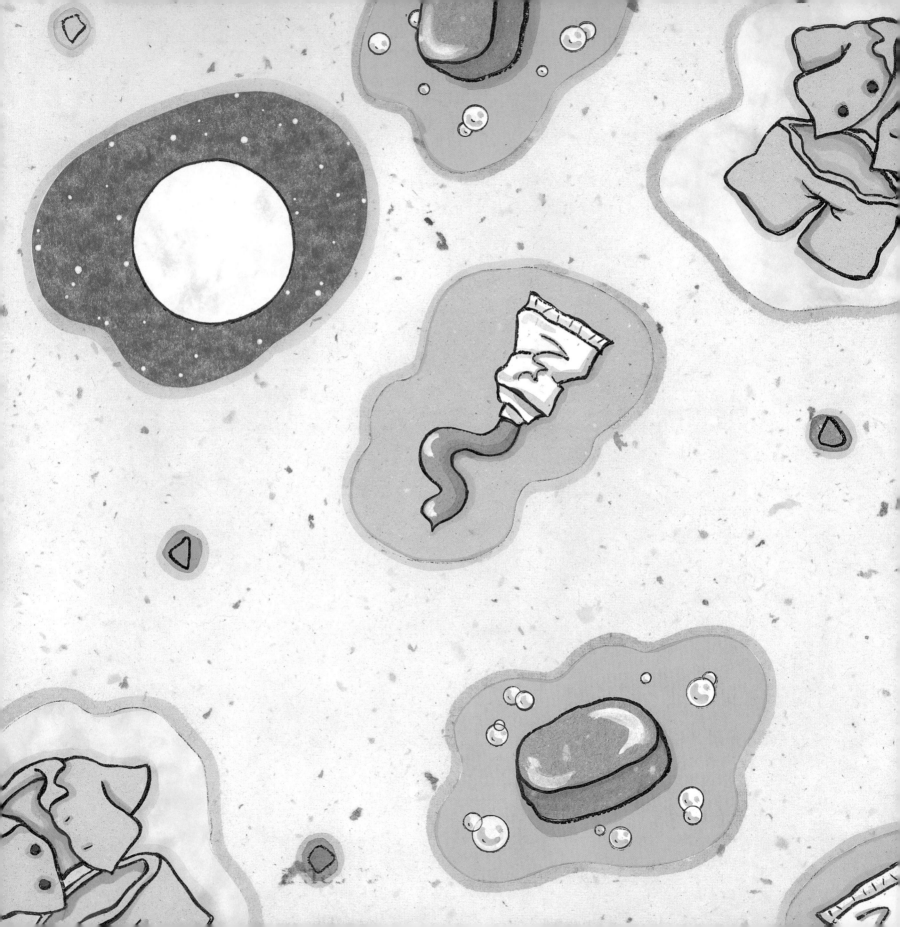

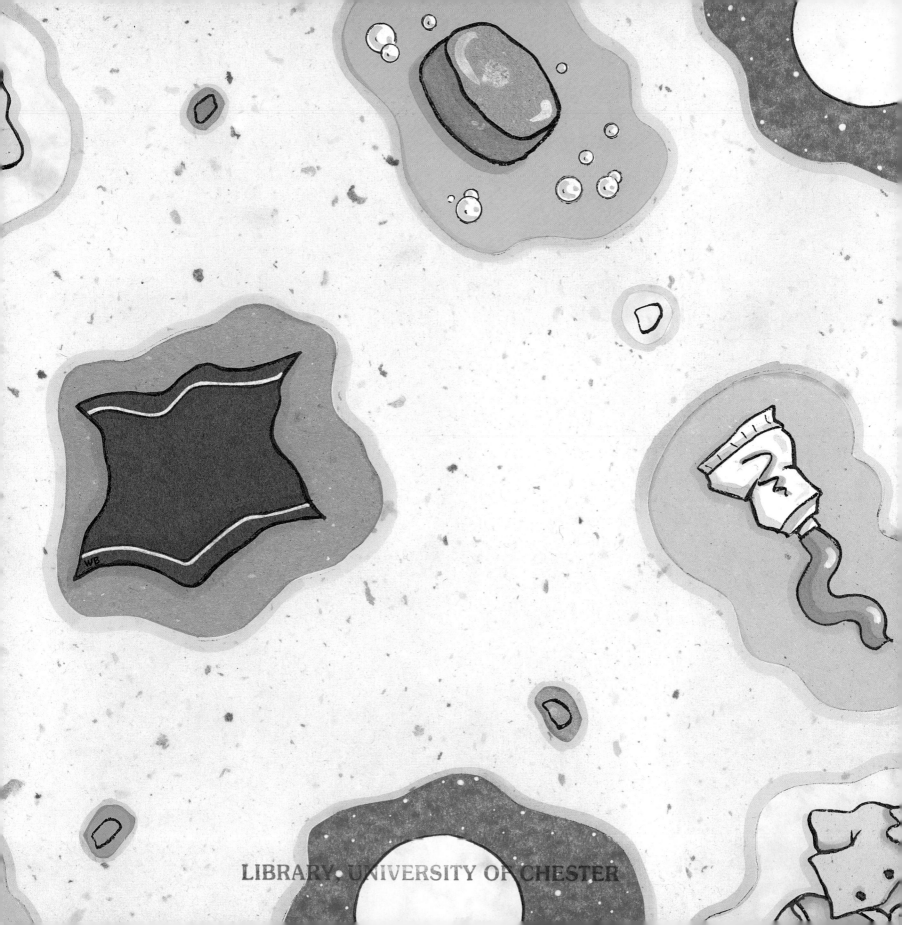